AF255178

The Jackdaw
and
The Doll

Illustrations

Izumi Yokoyama

Story

John Biscello

The Jackdaw and The Doll

Part I: Home

The time had come
for K. to spread his wings
and fly away from home
for the first time.

He would be leaving his birthplace,
The City of Velvet Fog.

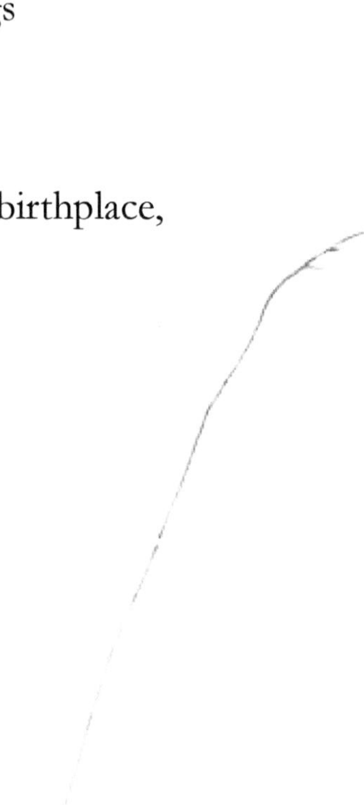

He would be leaving his family,
and the house where he had grown up.

He would be leaving his job as an office clerk,
the only job he had ever known.

K. knew the time had come
to expand his horizons
but a part of him, the little part,
wanted to ignore the clock
or freeze its hands.

You see, K. had fears.
Lots and lots of fears.

Braillovo pismo
Braille

Yet none of these fears were bigger
than what K. called The Shroud.
The Shroud was The Formless Thing
that had been stalking K. since childhood.

What did it want from him?
K. never knew.

There was only one thing that helped.
The night-flights.

Many years ago,
on the morning K. awoke
to find he had glossy gray-black feathers,
wings, a stubby black beak,
and crow's feet,
that was the day K. became
more than himself.
That was the day K. became a storyteller.

He began taking night-flights,
a jackdaw winging its way through velvety sheets of fog,
over bridges and cobbled streets,
past churches and castles,
gathering the stories
that he would bring home
when everyone was asleep.

In his room,
he would write
and write
and write,
and the mountain of pages
became his fortress and bravery
against The Shroud
and other fears.

When his family
found out about his night-flights,
they were greatly disturbed.
Especially his father,
a strict and sensible man.

Is my son mad?
Cursed?
A freak of nature?
Is this the devil's work?

K.'s father did not understand,
and in not understanding
he was scared
and forbid his son to take any more night-flights.

K., who feared his father
nearly as much as he feared The Shroud,
had never dared to disobey the man
who ruled with an iron hand.
But in this case he had no choice.
The voice inside calling him to fly
was more powerful than his father's commands.

So K. continued to fly every night,
and kept it hidden from his family.

K.'s double life went on like this for years,
timid clerk by day,
winged scribe by night,
and then two stirring forces
altered the course of his life.

Sickness.
And love.

When K. found out he was ill,
that dark liquid was rising inside his
chest,
he knew that drowning
at the hands of The Shroud
was his marked fate.

K.'s days grew longer,
          his night-flights shorter.

And then a new call to flying
came in the form of falling.
The lady K. fell in love with
was named Dora.

Dora loved K.
when he was timid,
when he was brave,
when he was night-flying,
when he was cowering
from The Shroud,
when he was lost in his pages,
when he was doing nothing at all,
simply still and soundless.

K. loved Dora in all her parts too.

K. and Dora decided to move
from The City of Velvet Fog
to The City of Birds,
a place where they both had always dreamed of living.

The time had come
for K. to spread his wings
and fly away from home
for the first time.

With Dora by his side.

Part II: Departure

As advertised,
The City of Birds
was filled with winged
species
of many kinds.

K. and Dora loved watching the birds
and taking walks in the park.
Sometimes in brief magical moments
they became children again.

There was paradise in slices
but there was also unrest
in a city where poverty, hunger and despair were on the rise,
much like the dark tide inside K's chest.

With each passing day,
K.'s breathing grew more and more labored.
His night-flights grew shorter and shorter
and then stopped altogether.

K. loved Dora with all his heart
but without the night-flights
he felt as if a part of him was shrinking
and feared that it would soon disappear completely.

K. now watched the birds
with soul-ache and grave longing.
He felt as if he were saying good-bye
to a truly golden part of his life.

And then, one day,
while strolling in the park,
he met the little girl
who renewed his strength
to fly again.

The little girl
sat on a park bench
crying big, splashy tears.

K. stopped and asked her what was wrong?

The little girl
said she had lost her doll
who was also her best friend.

"What's your name?" K. asked,
to which the girl responded, "Frieda."

"Ah, Miss Frieda, so you're the one!
You see, your doll is not lost,
she has simply gone off on an adventure."

"An adventure!?"
Frieda's eyebrows jumped.
"How do you know that?"

"I know because she sent me a letter."

"Really? Where is it?"

"I left it at home," K. explained,
"but if you meet me here tomorrow,
same time, same bench,
I will bring you the letter."

Frieda wiped away her tears
and thanked the man.
Then, looking down,
she noticed a single shiny black feather
covering the back of his hand.

"What's that?" Frieda asked.

K. blew the feather off
as it caught in the breeze
and whirled away.
Then he said, "Hope, Miss Frieda, that is hope."

When K. got home he told Dora
about the little girl he had met
and how he now had the sacred task
of writing a letter that would help her cope
with the loss of her best friend.

That night
K. flew
and tried to see
the city through the doll's
dream-fueled eyes.

When K. returned home
he was both exhausted and energized.
He stayed up all night
writing the letter
which spoke of the doll's
enchanting adventure.

The next day,
at the same time, on the same bench,
he met Frieda and gave her the letter.

Dearest Frieda, my Best of Best Friends,

I am sorry I left without saying good bye,
but it was time for me to go out into
the world and have a big adventure.
I miss you terribly

After reading the letter, Frieda wept.
She was both happy and sad.
When she wondered aloud
if she'd ever see her doll again,
K. said, "Well, I don't know if you'll see her,
but I do know you will hear from her again.
She promised another letter."

"She DID!?"
Frieda nearly jumped off the bench.

"Yes," K. said,
"same time tomorrow,
same bench."

And so,
over the course of the next two weeks,
K. flew nightly
and came home with stories
that he put in the letters
which he delivered to Frieda
every day,
same time, same bench.

Yet K. knew that all stories
must come to an end
and so he wondered
how the doll's story would finish.

Dora, who saw that K. was growing weaker
and weaker, his lungs and heart half-swallowed
in dark liquid, gave K. the key to an ending.

"Love," she said to him, "the story ends in love."

And so K. delivered the last letter
to Frieda, which broke the news—

When Frieda was done reading the letter,
she looked up at K., tears in her eyes,
and said, "I am happy for her.
Love sounds like a grand adventure, don't you think?"

K. agreed,
as tears welled in his eyes
and then rolled down his cheeks.

"Why are you crying?" Frieda asked.
K. looked deeply into Frieda's
sea-blue eyes lighted with innocence,
and then looked past Frieda,
as several leaves, yellow and brittle,
fell from a tree branch onto the grass.

"I'm crying, Miss Frieda," K. said,
because it has been an honor and a privilege
to have been your personal postman."

"Thank you," Frieda said,
and hugged K. for the first
and last time.

Three weeks later,
while K. was in his room writing,
a horned owl with large yellow
eyes
perched on the windowsill
and stared at K., unblinking.

Dora entered the room just as the owl
flew away, and she asked, "What was that?"

K. looked at her and whispered, "The bird of
death,"
and then went back to what he was writing.

Three days later
K. left behind the body
which had served him in sickness and in health.

The time had come for K.
to spread his wings
and expand his horizons
in a whole new way.

Part III: Return

You may not see him,
but know that there is
a ghost-bird flying nightly
through velvety sheets of fog,
over bridges and cobbled streets,
past churches and castles,
forever collecting stories
in which he finds himself
at home.

Afterword

The Jackdaw and the Doll was inspired by a story I first came across when reading Paul Auster's *The Brooklyn Follies*. Auster's protagonist relates the story of Franz Kafka's encounter with a young girl in a park in Steiglitz, a suburb in Berlin (Kafka had moved to Berlin in the autumn of 1923, where he lived with a woman named Dora Diamant). The girl is sorrow-stricken because she's lost her doll. Kafka explains to her that her doll is not lost at all, but rather has gone away on a trip. When the girl asks him how he knows that, Kafka tells her that the doll has written him a letter, and he will bring it to her tomorrow. And so begins Kafka's brief career as a "doll postman," as he delivers the girl a series of letters, sent by the girl's traveling doll, who is enjoying delightful adventures in different countries.

At the time, Kafka was very ill, in the twilight stages of the tuberculosis which would end his life the following spring, but, as the story goes, he didn't let his weakened condition stop him from putting great attention and care into the crafting of the doll-letters. The story ends with Kafka presenting the girl with a new doll, one which doesn't look the same as the girl's previous doll. This change in appearance is explained, in an attached note, which reads: "My travels have changed me…" The post-script to this story comes years later, when the girl, now an adult, discovers a slip of paper hidden inside a crevice in the doll's body. In short, it expressed: "Everything that you love, you will eventually lose, but in the end, love will return to you in a different form."

Is this story true? Was there really a young girl and a lost doll and a series of letters penned by Franz Kafka? No one knows for certain, though countless versions of the story, more or less following the same arc, have been shared. And oftentimes, the impact has been similar to the one I experienced when first reading the story in Auster's novel: a sense of being deeply touched and warmed inside, grace gently stirring the heart. Storytelling is a bridge to wonder and enchantment, to compassion and communion. It is also an alchemist, a healer, and a keeper of dreams. To have created a story, after reading a story about a man who devoted his soul to stories, reveals and honors the legacy of story-chains, and their quality of timelessness. Of course, words are only a part of this fable, and "Jackdaw" could not have realized the richness of its inspired flight without the brilliant artistry of Izumi Yokoyama. Yet another bridge, this one between words and images, in allowing for worlds to merge and harmonize.

Certain aspects of Kafka's life have also flavored and influenced this fable, such as his troubled relationship with his domineering father, his gnawing fears and anxieties, his passionate dedication to the written word. Then there's K's other self, "the jackdaw," a small bird belonging to the raven family. In the Czech Republic, this bird is known as "kavka," which also happens to be a variation on Kafka's surname.

Emily Dickinson spoke of "hope" as "that thing with feathers." May *The Jackdaw and the Doll* stand as a small, winged testament to such a golden claim.

J.B.

Izumi Yokoyama and John Biscello. Taos, NM. 2020

Izumi Yokoyama is a multi-media artist who lives and works in Taos, New Mexico. Born in Niigata, Japan, in 1980, Yokoyama graduated with an MFA from San Francisco Art Institute and moved to the high desert. Yokoyama's artwork, which has been presented locally and nationally, spotlights apparitional motifs while celebrating the juxtapositions of living and dying. The Japanese culture and desert stories significantly influence her creative process. She works in ink pen drawings, installations, murals, calligraphy, and interactive community projects.

Originally from Brooklyn, NY, novelist, poet, performer, and playwright, John Biscello, has called Taos, New Mexico home since 2001. He is the author of three novels: *Broken Land*, *Raking the Dust*, and *Nocturne Variations*; a collection of stories, *Freeze Tag*; two books of poetry, *Arclight* and *Moonglow on Mercy Street*, and an adaptation of classic folk tales, *Once Upon a Time: Classic Folktales Reimagined*.